This Book Belongs to:

....

Magical Stories

Featuring The Golden Goose, Chicken Little & the Little Mermaid

igloo

The Golden Goose

Once upon a time, there were three brothers. The two older brothers were clever and strong, but the youngest was small and shy.

One day, their father told them he needed some wood from the forest for the fire. The oldest and strongest brother jumped up. "I am the strongest and the smartest he said. I will go into the forest and bring back more wood than you'll ever need!"

So his mother gave the brother a loaf of freshly baked bread and a bottle of wine.

When the oldest brother reached the forest, he met an old man. "I am famished said the old man. Do you have any bread?"
"Yes," replied the brother, "but I need it for my own lunch. I cannot spare any."
"In that case," said the man, "do you have anything to drink?
"I'm sorry," said the brother. "I would give you some wine, but I need it for myself. Now, if you don't mind, I'm very busy, so I must be on my way!"

"It is a shame you cannot spare anything for me. Remember this if something happens to you," replied the old man mysteriously.

The oldest brother marched off into the forest and found a fine tree to chop. He had not been working long when CHIP! CHOP! OUCH! His hand slipped, and the axe cut him.
"Oh! Oh! My poor finger!" he cried. And he picked up his axe and ran home.

The next day, the second brother said, "I will take up the work of my injured brother." So he too was given a lunch of fresh bread and wine, and off he went to the forest to chop wood.

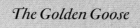

When he reached the forest, the second brother met the same old man. "Good day to you, young sir," smiled the old man. "Could you spare some of your lunch for a hungry old man?"

The second brother thought for a second. "I do have some bread," he replied, "but I surely cannot spare any." "Then maybe a little of your wine to ease my thirst?" asked the old man. "No," said the second brother. "You'll have to find some of your own."

"It is a shame you cannot spare anything for me. Remember this if something should happen to you," the old man replied.

With that, the brother marched off into the forest, and began work. CHIP! CHOP! OUCH! The axe slipped and struck him on the foot.

He let out a howl and hopped all the way home!

The next day, the youngest of the three brothers went to his father. "Let me go to chop wood for the fire," he said.

The older brothers mocked their younger sibling, and laughed that he would be too weak to chop the wood. But the family needed the wood, and so the youngest brother was sent on his way. There was no fresh bread left, and his older brothers had drunk all the wine, so all he was given was a piece of stale crust, and a flask of water from the well.

When the youngest brother reached the edge of the forest, he too met the little old man.
"Would you share your lunch with me?" the old man asked the boy.
"I only have stale old bread and water," replied the youngest brother, "but you are welcome to share it."

The old man thanked him. And when the boy took out the bread, it was as fresh as the morning it had been baked. What was more, the water had turned into sweet wine.

The old man turned to the boy.
"Because you have been kind to me, I will tell you a secret," he said, pointing to an old tree.

"Chop down that tree, and you will find something underneath it."

The youngest brother chopped down the tree. There, sitting among the roots, was a goose with feathers of pure gold.

The youngest brother knew that if he returned home, the goose would be taken away from him, so he found an inn where he could stay. The innkeeper had three daughters, and when they saw the goose, each one secretly decided they would wait for the right moment and then pluck one of the golden feathers.

Later that evening, when the boy was sleeping, the eldest of the daughters came and seized the goose. But when she tried to pull her hand away, she found that she could not remove a single feather. She was stuck fast!

Next came the second daughter. She too became stuck. The third sister came in soon after, and she got stuck as well.

The next morning, the boy awoke to find the innkeeper's three daughters attached to the golden goose. He picked up the goose and marched right out of the door, so that the daughters had to follow him wherever he decided to go. As he marched them through the streets of the village, they passed the church. "Dear me," cried the priest, who was standing outside. "What a shameful thing it is to see three girls chasing a poor boy. Let go of him, I beg you."

The priest he reached out to pull at the youngest daughter's sleeve as they passed by. But as he grabbed hold of her, he too became stuck fast.

The youngest son led the procession out of the village and into the fields, where they passed two farmers.

When the priest saw these big, strong men, he called out to them. "Please help! I'm stuck!"

So the farmers ran over and took hold of the priest.
But as soon as they did so, they too became fixed and had to follow

wherever they were led.

Soon the boy reached the city. The King who ruled the city had a beautiful daughter who was very sad. No one could cheer her up. In desperation, the King had put forth an order saying that any man who could make his daughter happy could have her hand in marriage.
As soon as the youngest of the brothers heard this, he went directly to the royal court, followed by the innkeeper's three daughters, the priest and the two farmers.

When the King's daughter witnessed this strange procession, she immediately burst into peals of laughter! The King, however, did not like the look of this silly boy and his goose, and changed his mind about the promise he had made.

"If you want to marry my daughter you must bring me a ship that can

sail on land and water!" he demanded, certain this time that the boy would fail.

But the boy was wiser than he looked. "The old man has helped me once," he thought to himself. "Why not a second time?"

He returned to the forest. He spoke to the old man.
"Because you are kind and generous, I will help you one last time," said the old man. In a flash there was a huge ship with wheels and sails, standing right next to them!

The youngest brother climbed aboard and sailed the ship all the way back to the city.

When the King saw this, he couldn't believe his eyes. But he knew there was nothing he could do. Reluctantly, he agreed at last to the marriage.

And so the youngest son, married a princess and became a royal prince. The brothers and parents of the youngest son begged his forgiveness for teasing him, and the son, being generous of heart, invited them to live in his kingdom. And so they all lived happily with each other for many years after.

Chicken Little

Chicken Little was wandering through the woods one day when PLOP, something small and hard fell onto her head. "Ouch," said Chicken Little. "That felt like the sky was falling." What Chicken Little had felt was an acorn falling from a tree, although she didn't know that.

She kept on walking when PLOP! PLOP! PLOP! Three acorns fell on her head all at once. "Help!" yelled Chicken Little. "The sky really is falling!"

As she was rushing along, she bumped into Henny Penny, who was out for a stroll.

"Help!" said Chicken Little to Henny Penny, "the sky is falling!"
"We must go to tell the King."
So, Chicken Little and Henny Penny set out to tell the King.

On the way, they met Ducky Lucky, who was going to the pond.
"Help!" said Henny Penny to Ducky Lucky. "The sky is falling!"
"Where?" asked Ducky Lucky, looking around in shock.
"Right on Chicken Little's head," said Henny Penny. "We must go to tell the King." So Chicken Little, Henny Penny and Ducky Lucky set out to tell the King.

On the way, they met Cocky Locky, who was going to the barnyard.
"Help!" said Ducky Lucky to Cocky Locky. "The sky is falling!"
"Where?" asked Cocky Locky, looking around in shock.
"Right on Chicken Little's head," said Ducky Lucky. "We must go to tell the King." So Chicken Little, Henny Penny, Ducky Lucky and Cocky Locky set out to tell the King.

On the way, they met Goosey Lucy, who was going to the market.
"Help!" said Cocky Locky to Goosey Lucy. "The sky is falling!"

"We must go to tell the King." So Chicken Little, Henny Penny, Ducky Lucky, Cocky Locky and Goosey Lucy set out to tell the King.

On the way, they met Turkey Lurkey, who was going to the meadow. "Help!" said Goosey Lucy to Turkey Lurkey. "The sky is falling!" "We must go to tell the King." So Chicken Little, Henny Penny, Ducky Lucky, Cocky Locky, Goosey Lucy and Turkey Lurkey set out to tell the King.

On the way, they met Foxy Loxy, who was going to his den. "Help!" said Turkey Lurkey to Foxy Loxy. "The sky is falling!" "Where?" asked Foxy Loxy, looking around in shock.

"Right on Chicken Little's head," said Turkey Lurkey. "We must go tell the King."

But Foxy Loxy said that if the sky was falling, they would be safer waiting in his den until the danger was over. So Chicken Little, Henny Penny, Ducky Lucky, Cocky Locky, Goosey Lucy and Turkey Lurkey all followed Foxy Loxy into his den.

But of course it was not safe in the den and the danger was far from over, for Foxy Loxy gobbled up Chicken Little, Henny Penny, Ducky Lucky, Cocky Locky, Goosey Lucy and Turkey Lurkey. And the King never did find out that the sky was falling.

The Little Mermaid

Far beneath the clear blue waves, the Little Mermaid lived in her father's kingdom with her five sisters and her grandmother.

The Little Mermaid loved to listen to her grandmother as she told tales of the world above the sea. She was mesmerized by her grandmother's descriptions of human beings and their ships, of the birds that flew high in the sky and the busy towns by the seashore. But the Little Mermaid couldn't discover these things for herself; for a mermaid had to be fifteen before she was allowed to rise to the surface to see these extraordinary sights.

The Little Mermaid waited impatiently for her fifteenth birthday.

On the day she turned fifteen, she could barely contain her excitement as she held on to her sisters hands and they started to swim towards the surface.

As her head popped above the waves for the first time, the Little Mermaid gasped – for the sun's rays glittered on the water and the clouds glowed pink and gold. It was the most beautiful thing the Little Mermaid had ever seen.

Suddenly, the peaceful scene was shattered by a loud explosion. There before her was a ship, lit up by fireworks in the sky. Laughter drifted across the water.

On board the ship a party was under way to celebrate a young Prince's birthday. The Little Mermaid watched as the humans danced on the deck. She gazed at the handsome Prince and imagined herself twirling around in his arms.

As the celebrations went on, the calm seas gave way to waves. They were gentle at first, but the wind grew stronger and soon huge waves were crashing onto the decks of the boat. With a terrifying groan, the deck split in two and the ship began to break up in the swirling waters.

The Little Mermaid watched in horror as the handsome young Prince was thrown into the churning sea. At first he swam against the waves, but soon he grew tired and slipped beneath the surface. Down, down, down he sank.

"I must save him," cried the Little Mermaid. With a flick of her tail, she dived beneath the heaving waves and scooped up the young man in her arms.

She held the Prince tightly in her arms and allowed the waves to carry them towards the shore. The Little Mermaid stayed with the Prince on the beach for as long as she dared, singing to him softly. But as the sun's rays grew stronger, she knew that she had to return to the water.

The Little Mermaid could not stop thinking about the handsome Prince. Every day she sat on the rocks in the bay to watch him walking in the palace gardens. At first this was enough, but after a while she longed to speak with him.

"But that will never happen," she sighed. "I'll never be human."

"You could be, if you wanted," said a voice next to her. The Little Mermaid turned to find herself face to face with a Sea Fairy. The Little Mermaid hesitated. Sea Fairies were always trouble! But then again, she did seem to know of a way that the Little Mermaid could be human . . .

Ignoring her doubts, the Little Mermaid followed the Sea Fairy.

"I have a potion that will change your tail into legs so you can walk with your Prince," cackled the Sea Fairy. "If you can make him fall in love with you before the sun sets on the second day, you will become human forever. If you fail, you will become a mermaid once more, but must serve me for all eternity!"

The Little Mermaid nodded her agreement as the Sea Fairy passed her a small bottle containing the powerful potion.

The Little Mermaid swam slowly towards the surface with the potion bottle held tightly in her hand. Finally she reached the shore, and sat on the sandy beach below the palace on the cliff. With trembling hands, she uncorked the potion. It smelled terrible!

Shutting her eyes, she put the bottle to her lips and quickly drank the liquid. Her throat burned and her eyes watered, but it was soon forgotten as the Little Mermaid saw her tail change before her very eyes into two pale legs. Very slowly, she stood up and took her first wobbly steps.

Meanwhile, at the palace, the Prince was gazing far out to sea, thinking about the mysterious girl who had rescued him.

"All I can remember is that she had a beautiful singing voice," he told his servant. "If only I could find her. I long to hear her voice again."

Just then, the Prince's servant spotted a bedraggled girl walking up the cliff path. "She must be a survivor from the shipwreck," cried the Prince. "Bring her into the palace and take care of her." He did not recognize the Little Mermaid.

The Little Mermaid was overjoyed. But her happiness was short-lived. The Prince's parents wanted him to marry a princess.

With a heavy heart, the Little Mermaid retired to her bed. It seemed that tomorrow she would have return to the sea to spend her days serving the Sea Fairy.

As dawn broke the next day, a fanfare announced the arrival of the Princess's ship. The Little Mermaid watched from her balcony as the sails grew larger on the horizon. Seeing the Princess, the Little Mermaid was filled with dismay.

She was very beautiful. Her golden, silky hair shone in the sunshine and her eyes sparkled as she gazed at the Prince. The Little Mermaid was certain she had lost her Prince forever.

Celebrations lasted for the rest of the day, but the Little Mermaid could not join in. How could she celebrate, when her Prince was to marry another? Soon the sun would dip behind the horizon, and she must return to the sea to become a slave.

Suddenly the Little Mermaid heard a splash. She looked up, it was her sisters!

"All is not lost," they told her, when they heard their sister's tale. "We heard the Prince's servant say his master longs to hear the voice of the girl who rescued him. You must sing, sing with all your heart!"

So, as the sun began to set, the Little Mermaid sang the song she had sung to the Prince on the beach. The haunting melody drifted across the sands to where the Prince was standing. At once, he rushed over to the Little Mermaid and embraced her.

"It was you who saved me," he cried, planting a kiss her on her cheek. "I have searched for you everywhere! I will never let you go again!"

Just at that moment, the sun dipped behind the horizon. The spell was broken and the Little Mermaid's wish had come true – she would be human forever and stay with her handsome Prince.